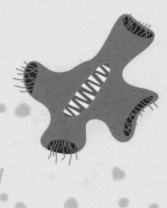

Ken's STICKY-ICKY OOEY-GOOEY YUCKY-SUCKY germy hands

written by **Glenda LaBassiere**
illustrated by **Penny Weber**

ISBN 978-0-578-96761-5

For my precious granddaughter,
Kennedy Alexandria Outram

Drawing on the sidewalk with
my brother Lux was so much fun!

We used jumbo chalk to draw
silly pictures and shapes.

We ran into the kitchen to get a snack.
When I reached for my favorite goldfish crackers,

Mommy said, "No, no, no — let's wash the chalk
off your hands first!"

"But why?" I asked. "It's just chalk!"

Mommy said, Germs are tiny bacteria that live
all around us.

"Bacteria? What's that?" I asked.

Mommy said bacteria are tiny germs
we can only see with a microscope.

When our hands are not clean,
germs can get into our tummy
and make us sick.

"Twenty seconds of washing
for clean hands," Mommy said.

"How will we know when
20 seconds is up?"
asked Ken.

"We sing,"
said Mommy.

(Sing to the melody of "Happy Birthday" and then repeat.)

Let's wash, wash our hands
with water and soap.
Warm water and soap
will wash germs away.
Warm water and soap
can wash germs away.
Scrub fingers and nails
to keep germs away.

I loved to help Mommy plant flowers
in her patio garden.

I used a small scoop shovel to put the dirt in.
Lux helped pat the dirt down.

"Oh, no! Look at our hands!" I said.

Mommy said, "It's okay, we can wash away
the dirt with soap and water."

"Germs are everywhere,"
Mommy said, "even in
a beautiful garden!

Remember:
20 seconds for clean hands.

Come on, let's sing."

(Sing to the melody of "Happy Birthday" and then repeat.)

Let's wash, wash our hands with water and soap.

Warm water and soap will wash germs away.

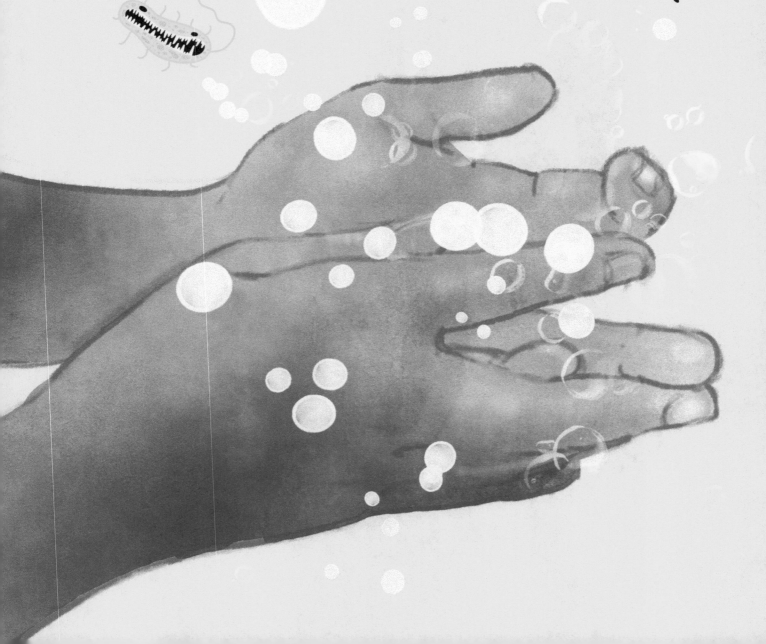

Warm water and soap
can wash germs away.

Scrub fingers and nails
to keep germs away.

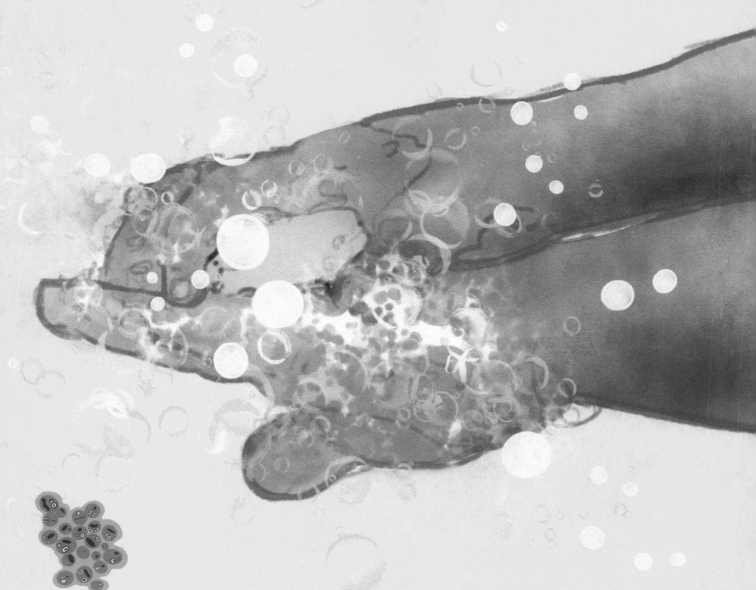

Saturday was my favorite day of the week because I got to be Mommy's special helper in the kitchen.

We picked blueberries from the garden
to bake my favorite dessert,
blueberry pie.

I watched as Mommy lay the ingredients
on the table.

I couldn't wait to get started.
"Before we begin," Mommy said,
"we have to wash our hands."

"Look, my hands are clean!" I said.

Mommy took my hands and spoke in her soft whisper voice.

"Anything we touch can have germs on it. We don't want them in our food, so when we prepare food we need clean hands.

Twenty seconds for clean hands. Come on, let's sing."

(Sing to the melody of "Happy Birthday" and then repeat.)

Let's wash, wash our hands with water and soap.

Warm water and soap will wash germs away.

Warm water and soap
can wash germs away.

Scrub fingers and nails
to keep germs away.

When I visited Aunt Gigi and Aunt Deiya,
it was so much fun.

Aunt Gigi let me play with her cute bunny
named Thumper.

Thumper loves carrots.

Aunt Deiya let me feed
snacks to Marz,
the family dog.

"Pets also carry germs," Aunt Gigi said,
"so, we always wash our hands after playing
with Thumper and Marz.

Twenty seconds for clean hands.

Come on, let's sing."

Let's wash, wash our hands
with water and soap.

Warm water and soap
will wash germs away.

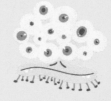

Warm water and soap
can wash germs away'

Scrub fingers and nails
to keep germs away'

We took an afternoon walk to the park.

I liked when Mommy watched me slide down fast!

Lux liked when Daddy pushed him on the swing.

When we got home from the park,
Mommy said,

"Germs live everywhere, even at the park."

I looked at my hands, "Oh, no!
Sticky-icky, ooey-gooey, yucky-gucky,
germy hands!"

"Let's all wash our hands.
Twenty seconds for clean hands.

Come on, let's sing."

Warm water and soap
can wash germs away.

Scrub fingers and nails
to keep germs away.

"Hooray!"

shouted Ken. "I have clean hands.

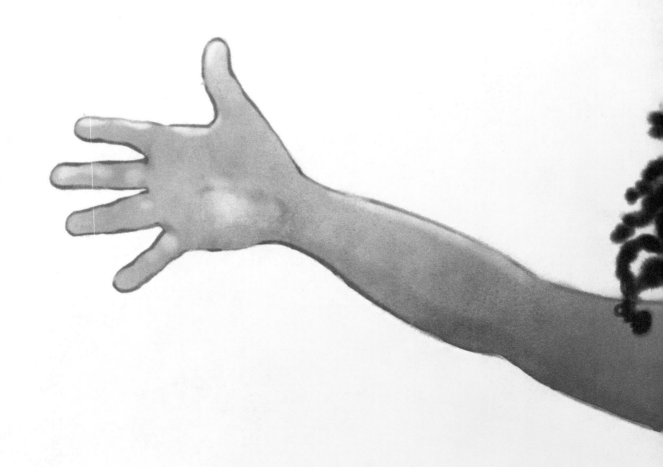

No more

sticky-icky, ooey-gooey, yucky-gucky, germy hands!"

What Can You Do Ooey-gooey, Yucky-

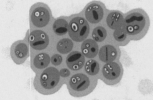

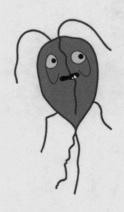

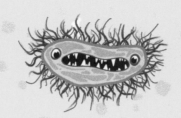

About Sticky-icky, gucky, Germs

Germs are tiny living things that can only be seen with a microscope.

When the bad germs (bacteria or virus) get inside your body, sometimes they multiply and make you sick.

Your hands pick up germs when you touch things that are contaminated.

We can't avoid germs, but we can prevent them from getting into our bodies by washing our hands with warm water and soap.

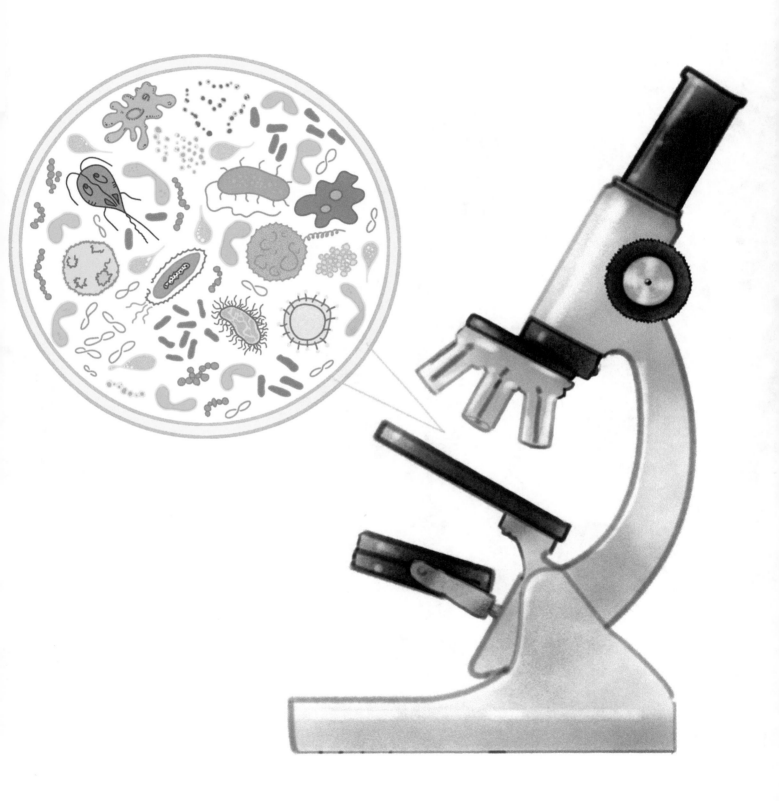

Germs spread through the air when
you cough or sneeze.

When you breathe the air, germs can get into your lungs
and make you sick.

Cover your cough or sneeze into your elbow.
This way you can keep your hands germ-free.

No one wants yucky-gucky, germy hands!

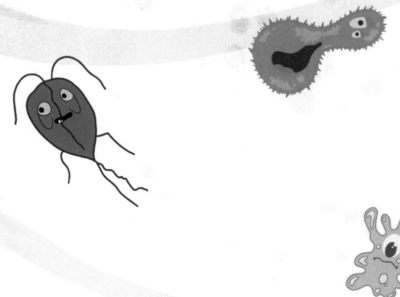

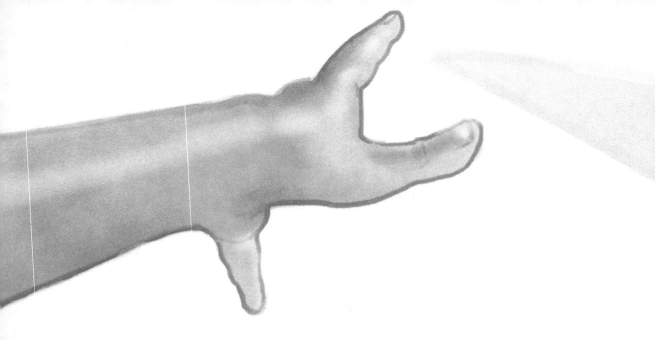

When you have the sniffles, don't rub your
nose on your arm!

Germs can get inside your body if you
have cuts or bruises.

Use a tissue, then toss the germy tissue in the trash.

No one wants sticky-icky, germy hands!

Germs live on objects everywhere,
even at school.

Your skin prevents germs from entering
your body, but germs can make you sick
if they get in your
eyes, nose, or mouth.

Keep your hands away from your face.

No one wants
ooey-gooey, germy hands!

Germs like to hide in bathrooms.

Yuck!

Always wash your hands when you are
finished using the bathroom.

Bacteria and virus can make you very sick
when they get inside your body.

Remember, if you don't want
sticky-icky, ooey-gooey, yucky-gucky, germy hands,
all you have to do is wash, wash, wash,
to keep the germs away!

Twenty seconds for clean hands.

Come on, let's sing one more time.

(Sing to the melody of "Happy Birthday"
and then repeat.)

Let's wash, wash our hands
with water and soap.
Warm water and soap
will wash germs away.

Warm water and soap
can wash germs away.

Scrub fingers and nails
to keep germs away.

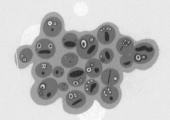

Glenda LaBassiere works as an educator with
the New York City Department of Education.
She holds a M.S. Ed in Early Childhood
Education, and B.A in Psychology.

She's married and has three adult daughters.
Glenda lives in Brooklyn, New York,
with her family.

Glenda loves cooking and baking. When she's not
in the kitchen, you can find her listening to
gospel music which is one of her pastime.

This is her first children's book.

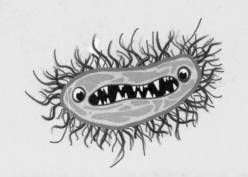